SEP   2012

PIG
HAS A PLAN

by Ethan Long

Holiday House / New York

To Azalia and Amir.
Love, Uncle Stinky

I LIKE TO READ is a registered trademark of Holiday House, Inc.
Copyright © 2012 by Ethan Long
All Rights Reserved
HOLIDAY HOUSE is registered in the U.S. Patent and Trademark Office.
Printed and Bound in March 2012 at Tien Wah Press, Johor Bahru, Johor, Malaysia.
The text typeface is Report School.
The artwork was created with black Prismacolor colored pencils
on bristol board and colored digitally on a Mac.
www.holidayhouse.com
First Edition
1 3 5 7 9 10 8 6 4 2
Library of Congress Cataloging-in-Publication Data
Long, Ethan.
Pig has a plan / by Ethan Long. — 1st ed.
p. cm. — (I like to read)
Summary: Pig is trying to take a nap, but his friends
are making all kinds of noise.
ISBN 978-0-8234-2428-3 (hardcover)
[1. Naps (Sleep)—Fiction. 2. Noise—Fiction. 3. Pigs—Fiction.
4. Domestic animals—Fiction.] I. Title.
PZ7.L8453Pi 2012
[E]—dc23
2011041294

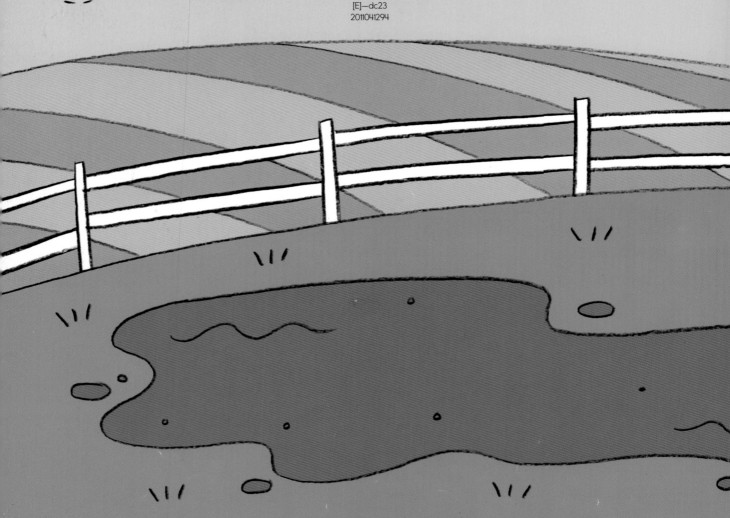

Pig wants to nap.

Hen wants to saw.

Cow wants to gab.

Cat wants to pop.

Dog wants to tap.

Rat wants to mix.

Hog wants to hum.

Pup wants to bop.

Pig has a plan.

Now Pig can nap.